Wonders of Sky

Warisha Yunus Ansari

FanatiXx Publication

AM/56, Basanti Colony, Rourkela 769012, Odisha
ISO 9001:2015 CERTIFIED
Website: *www.fanatixx.in*

"WONDERS OF SKY"

By: **WARISHA YUNUS ANSARI**

ISBN: 978-93-89557-56-5

English & Hindi Poetry & Quotes

1st Edition

BOOK FORMATTING: JAPNEET KAUR
BOOK COVER: SAGAR SAMAL
PRESENTED BY: REASONS AND LAUGHTER

DISCLAIMER

This is a work of fiction. Our editors have tried their best to edit the content of all the author/authors and check the plagiarism. All the write-ups in this book are unique and are only published in this book.
In case any plagiarism or error is found, the author is the sole responsible and not the publisher.

Acknowledgement

I am eternally thankful to almighty for giving me strength, wisdom and And an opportunity to showcase my pieces to the world in the form of my words.

I'm blessed to be the daughter of such a supportive parents who never let me down and encourages me to fulfil all my lil-big dreams.

Couldn't be less thankful to Japneet Kaur for providing me a platform to accomplish my first dream anthology book.

A hearty and warm thanks to all the co-author for their beautiful write ups, poems, quotes and short story and for their constant support and patience.

Thanks A Lot to everyone who encouraged me for turning the "Wonders Of Sky" into reality.

This book is a masterpiece of all the wonderful co-author with their wonderful write ups,
Involving all the Love, Hope and Peace.

About The Compiler

Warisha Ansari from Mumbai, Persuading 12th from Science field. Loves to Read, Write and Sing (Wrong lyrics) Co-author of 10+ anthologies. Reading and Writing has been her favourites since she was 8. Runs on Stationary, Love and Humanity. Always found on Instagram admiring poets and daydreaming about being the one @_imperfect_ink. Watch life through the lens. Photography and Calligraphy are the other activities she puts her interest in. Life has been a tragedy but she keep going on a mantra that "What's your will find you". A simple girl who tries to make herself and others happy through her poems and lame jokes.

FOUNDER

JAPNEET KAUR

Japneet Kaur, daughter of Mr. Surjeet Singh and Mrs. Dilpreet Kaur was brought up in Indirapuram, UP. She is pursuing German language and BA programming course from Delhi University. She is a passionate writer who loves to pen down her emotions and environment and strive to make her parents proud. She is even working on her very first novel making her one step closer to her goal.

Instgram : @sheedreamss

EDITOR

PHALGUNI JAGADEESH

""There are many ways to achieve something in life and knowing the purpose of living, I got mine through words."

She is from Tamil Nadu, she has completed her MBA in Marketing and HR. Writing was her hobby once upon a time which has become her profession now. She is a passionate writer who loves to ink her emotions without any flaws. She is a free verse writer and also has invented two of her own poetry forms. Reasons and Laughter has given her a great platform to explore, learn and improve herself in all possible ways.

Instagram : @phal_candy & @pjinklings

HINDI EDITOR

SHASHWAT A. TRIVEDI

"Expressing the feelings in words is something I do."
Shashwat, currently a technical student with a hobby of writing. And trying to express the things which will last for a longer period of time, as I can't be universal but I want my words to justify my name which simply means universal.

A poet, writer, and a performer as well.

Performed in approx 20 events and wrote for around 10 anthologies.

Love to express in my native language, so I write and perform in Hindi.

Instagram handle : @shashwat_trivedi31

DESIGNER

SAGAR SAMAL

Sagar Samal is a Photographer, Image Manipulation and Colour Grading Artist.
Hardworking with a "Create Something Awesome" Mentality.
A graduate in Bachelor of Computer Application but an Artist By Heart.

Instagram : photosign.cf

POEMS

Warisha Ansari

//Glad I met you//

For me ' I love you'
has turn out to be just words
the feelings they used to give
has been killed brutally
by the person I loved the most.

Then I heard the same words
from you too
maybe it's the 88th time
for someone is showing me the love
but this one sounds like-
a raindrop
a ray of hope
a rose that smells like forever
a lie- a beautiful lie
that I wish to hear for the rest of my life.

After a long time,
when you promised me
the world and hereafter
I whispered in my heart
'Please stay, I need you maybe.'
When you say

"You are send in my life for a purpose"
I wish upon the every possible star that purpose is
to hold your hand and
travel the whole world,

I wish that purpose is to
watch the best of my life
from your eyes,
I wish that purpose is to
catch me whenever I fall,
I wish that purpose is to
make me believe in love again.

But then,
The nightmare of what the future hold haunts me,
It makes me cry the ocean of tears
thinking about the 'what ifs'
I'm afraid of losing you
and so I'm afraid of losing
the every bit of pieces
I shared with you.

Also then,
Whatever the future holds
I Promise
I'll remember you
In my prayers,
In my dreams,
In the curves
you bring on my face
even when my muscles
refuse to move.
There will be your traces
In the pages of my diary.
There will be you
Somewhere inside my heart, making me happy:)

<u>Isha Singhal</u>

<u>///Newborn love!///</u>

Yeah, I remember that late night hug,
Made me feel alive and loved,
The shattered pieces started coming back together,
It was windy and my kinda weather,
He was wearing black shirt,
She put on her favourite red top,
Both were complementing each other.

The sky turned dark as they hold hands,
And moon witnessed her love for him,
Meanwhile, the stars celebrated their love.
But that was the peace before a thunderstorm,
She was totally unaware of the horn,
The car of life hit her bad,
And she lost that precious one she never had.

Simran Arora

///It's never too late//

Life is a merry-go-round,
With me on it
Holding its hands
Tight enough to fall.
I can feel the breeze,
The chills of the windy trees,
Having me puzzled
With origin of the blow,
Is it the fluttering trees?
Sun is ready for its evening fall,
Disappearing in its cloak
But it is not dark yet
I can still have a walk.

<u>*Aritra Kundu*</u>

<u>//Gems //</u>

Every year adds new people to life,
Some turn into your own very swiftly,
And some take time to open up.
It's not about which type of person;
You meet in that time frame,
It's all about the one who make it,
Worth living every possible time.
Yes people leave when it's done,
And with it the burden of expectations,
Leave us sore to the core.
We can't force everyone to hung up,
Because who wish to leave will go
Anyways without thinking much about you,
So stop the surge of expectations
That one raises with the people they have,
Rather live the life with the one who
Actually want to stand with you
Without any reason behind,
These are the actual gems whom,
You can't lose in any time frame,
They will always bring back,
The lost shine again no matter,
How dull the situation is!!

Shraddha Cholera

//War for Love//

Of course he is mine,
I begged you for us,
but you just stonewalled my prayers
Of course he is mine,
And that reason is enough for war with you.
I challenge you,
write his name in my destiny otherwise,
"Just be ready"

Banasmita Behera

//Home...The Heaven on Earth//

There is no place like home,
Where there's smell of acceptance
and where we feel our existence.

The aroma of love in the air
gives the sense of belonging,
The respect we are longing
Finally someone takes care.

We can hear the caring voice
Which pulls us like magnet,
Burying the dreaded hatchet
We talk, make merry and rejoice.

We have a lot of places to roam,
But there is no place like home

Manha Siddiqui

///LET'S TRY///

Let's take a step towards our destiny
It won't be very easy, I know honey!
But I heard someone saying,
The first step is a hard travelled a mile.
Do something creative and new
Like it's just made for you.
Learn from experience
For the upcoming be curious It may hurt
But that's what life is.
Mistakes you'll do a lot
But there's always a second chance you have got.
Set your goals high
And as long as you try
Your goals will never seem high.

///Seashore///

Sitting on the seashore
I see
It's beautiful to watch the waves crashing
on the sand and seagulls soar,
The place is silent
Though it says it all..

It tells stories about shells and rocks..
And as soon as on the seashore I walk
It's the waves with whom ceaselessly I talk..
It's the place where I badly cried
The place that cleans the troubles of my mind..

I listen to the talks of the waves
Which call themselves as brave.
I told them they are something mysterious and strange
Something the mother nature claims .

As I leave the place I pray ,
Until my next visit
The place remains the same.

//STORM //

The sky is full of black clouds
Too dark it is out
Looks like the cotton balls above to want to cry
Thunder roars at its loudest of sound
Seems that they too have some secret wounds..
Cold breeze passes through her hair
As she stands stock still
Gazing at the sky
Wanting to cry
Or maybe to run..
Run away to a place that doesn't exist
Rain drops that drizzled resembles the tear that had fallen from her
eye

She's lost.
She's lost in a world of her own away from the reality,all alone
Or maybe in a place surely not for the givers of pain
A place where no one is blamed to have scars and stains.
She's lost.
She's still in her oblivion of her world insensible of the storm .

///I'LL RISE//

Talk bitter about me
Say lies, put me in dirt
But darling
I'll rise !!
You see me broken
You know I too cry
Wanting for more?
Bitch please out of your mess
I'll rise!!
You target me with your hatred full eyes,
Or with the not so truthful lies
But I know I'll still rise !
Because I learnt through you
I learnt how to face the fear
I learnt how to bear
Leave behind the regrets and pain
I learnt how to rise like the sun and be nourishing like the rain ..
After all the dirt you had put on my name
I'll rise
I'll still rise!!

Mohammad Umar M

//The sweetest friend//

Just as I was passing through,
The sweet shop by the road.
I could smell the sweetness
Of all the sweets swarming my nose.

I stood there for sometime
Just imagining the sweetness and,
How people are addicted to it.
The way every sweet is unique.

I could just imagine my best friend
Thinking how lucky I am
To have my friend in life
That spreads sweetness in my life.

Imagining how sweet my best friend is,
Sweet like rasgulla,
Aroma like halwa,
Satisfactory like barfi.

Just feeling my bestie and,
The sweetness that brings to me
The happiness it brings in my life
The smile it brings to my face.

I was satisfied with my best friend
So I did not feel the need
To go buy and have a sweet
When I already have a sweetest friend.

<u>Priyambada Behera</u>

<u>//Healer //</u>

You are not here
Still you are here
My eyes look for you
My heart craves for you
My soul longs for you
I wish to be with you
I live for you
My love is only you
You are an open book
And I'm messed trap
You are the healer to my pain
Pain Killer to my pain
You are a never ending journey
As sweet as honey
Idol of my life
I wish to be your wife
The boy of my dream
The only hope in gloom
Am Ur missing peace
And you are my sunshine
I am the page with lots of cuts and scratches
You are the page to new begin
The more I think
The most I fall in love with you
You are my strength
And you are the only one I want to be with.

Karthika Padmakumar

//Why? //

Why do I run back to you?
Its always you, don't know why.
You are always there for me,
Like you are my savior, I look upto you.

We are inevitable, a perfectly found
Star-crossed friendship we share.
A mutual feeling, a bond so strong,
We can barely part, even for a day.

We love each other in friendship,
Being together makes us strong.
We can't separate for we are one,
The two that are meant to be.

Mohammad Ahmed

//Matter of Seconds//

In a matter of seconds, I lost myself.
I saved a life, and that something gained redeemed it.
Not my own life, I can't draw to save my own life.
And now I sit endlessly listening to the same love song.
I was never a believer of love at first sight.
But from now on I just might endlessly I listen to the same love song,
like its oxygen.
Finding lost courage to hunt for lost butterflies.
To awake from the bed of regret that doesn't matter anymore.
I recite the chorus; the tense part to stimulate the instruments of my
heart.
To alleviate the aching of my soul and tame the tempest that wilts my
innocence.
Same love song, it is a pain to love; we crave the affection of someone
we can't have.
They've chosen someone else, or have passed.
We cradle ourselves in a bed of regret, of what ifs.
To find meaning and closure in what used to matter.
When in reality it doesn't matter anymore, we need to move on.
Maybe I need to too.

//Intoxication//

It was an exotic marvel, a fantastic short-lived tale.
A treasure unshared with humankind.
A devastation that would terminate –
-alienate and burn to ashes any existing relationships.
A ritual that manipulated love and alternated history,
A phenomenon that would faux pas one's' destiny –

-to nepenthe one's elegy and pledge serenity.
It was dirty child's play on a god's scale.
The becoming of an unstoppable cult that –
-saturated the purity of love and terraformed it into a wildlife.
Like wild horses, it tamed two beings to perform unspeakable acts.

An urban legend, we know it as Black magic.
How tragic, centuries and still it has been discovered.
It was the devils beloved elixir.

Aayushi Gupta

//Falling Star//

We're all just seeds,
trying to bloom into long and green plants.
We're all just crescents,
longing to be a full moon.
We're all just that last passenger on the bus,
waiting for his destination to come.
But alas, it never does!
All of this never happens.
Because there are too many obstacles on this way.
Stopping us,
making us struggle,
leaving us behind in the race.
These try to test us.
But we lose.
We always lose miserably.
Even though we don't want to, but we do.
As it's fated.
We aren't the winners.
We're the strugglers in this life full of thorns.
Each thorn pricks us,
we always bleed.
Our skin is cut open every time,
but we never heal.
We just be.
And that is why;
The flower never blooms.
The full moon night never comes.
The bus always keeps moving.
And we,
We remain right where we started,
Right there,
Sitting beside our windows,
Staring up at the night sky,
Waiting for a falling star.

Lakshita Shirmali

// Tom and Jerry//

Some dreams can never come true
Your words I admire
I don't know why destiny allows some people to meet
When no one among them can desire

Heart, Beats, Fast, Colours
And promises
How to be brave
How can I love when I am afraid

You and I again and again
Always almost never enough
Tom and Jerry maybe kiddish
But the be the Relation which I love

I love you, but u made me blue
Still do when I don't have a clue
After all u give me hue
Because all I want it's you I just wish you knew

I want to tell you that
You mean everything to me
I am just afraid to hear that I mean nothing to you
I have died everyday waiting for you
Darling don't be afraid I have loved you!

Mamta Bhagat

//Hey U girl!//

How much I love You
Is what I can't explain
Also, if I treat u bad
Still I can't see you in Pain.

You are my friend who turns to
Where my soul needs a lift
Your friendship is something I treasure
For true Friendship is a Gift.

You know baby how much do I care
I feel the best when You are there .
For you I have special kinda Devotion
Which best signifies my Love and Emotion.

I will prove my Friendship
Even if stops the world
Like that elastic rubber
Which never wants to curl.

We always still together till the end
Our friendship is like a straight line that will never bend...

We together have a special kinda Grace
Where we are In
That's the coolest place!

You have advised me to do things I like
You have helped me to do things Alike!

Life is awesome when you are around
There is the smell of love that purely surrounds.
I still search for You in Crowds;
In empty fields and soaring clouds.

When I feel low about myself
You will always be the one to give me the best help
So Lastly,
Stay as u r Oh! My pretty Soul
Cuz my life goes on the movie of your awesome ROLE!!

Arihana Saikia

//Left behind//

The clear, quiet vicinity
And a view through the height
I hardly have any picture in thought
'Cause that's all I left behind

The tranquillity
And the things I had in mind
A vision of a tree and me playing around
It's what I left behind

A paved path
Where roses were lined
Now a blurred image
And I left it behind

Paddling through the stones
And the houses that I remind
A thought of their owners
Whom I left behind

I wish I could stay
And be a little kind
To go back
To what I left behind.

<u>Kshama Rao</u>

///HOPE//

Hope is positive,
It is a magic carpet,
Don't give up,
Don't lose hope,
There is no cure like hope,
Hope feeds,
We are alive because of hope,
Hope is like stars in the darkness,
I hope this inspires everyone.

QUOTES

Japneet Kaur

-'15 days up and you didn't even call him. I guess you are competing
with his ego'

Friend taunted

'Just trying to choose myself over him'

her tears smiled

-Don't get close to me,
I love too much.
And when you leave killing every piece of me, which was left in me
leaving me scattered,
I feel empty and numb.
I feel as if now nothing is left in me which I can call mine,
And at the end, it's only me who gets hurt too much,
If you don't deserve too much love, don't get close to me.

-How ironical it is!
When the whole world is trying to break you
Still you're so strong to let it flow over you,
But then,
You meet this one person,
Whom you consider your whole world and when he tries to break
you,
You lose it completely.

- The sayings you love our just the spilled pain on the sheet of paper
in words.

Phalguni Jagadeesh

-Don't expect anything from anyone.

A slight change will also hurt you.

Expectation always gives you pain.

-Don't expect anything from anyone.

A slight change will also hurt you.

Expectation always gives you pain.

-Silence says a lot.

It's just that people with us should understand.

Chaos mind will just ruin things,

Take some time out, think and proceed.

-A deep breathe,
Some silence,
Thoughts running in mind,
Music,
Inking words,
Letting out the emotions,
Peaceful sleep.

Solace!!

Things which are priceless.

Mehnaaz shaik

-That spark in his eyes slits up the darker wisps of her soul .

-Heartbreak doesn't matter when the fire in you is bright enough to lighten up your path.

-The pain on my lips reminds me of that potent taste .

-His love was like a breeze which blows through her heart and soothes her soul .

<u>*Charu Sharma*</u>

-I have hope.
Hope that everything comes out to the best.
With all the mess that's life's been creating,
I'm waiting for the sunrise to arrive.
And my life to shine again, bright.

-The love I had for you..
It's still the same.
I just stopped pretending,
because I know you will not love me the same.
Like you did before.

-There's a mess inside my heart,
and I want separation but I can't.
I'm stuck in a situation which I hope that it would surpass.

<u>Vishva Gajjar</u>

-You know what breaks the heart
more than love?
When you have a lot to share
but no one to listen.

-Your memories are
too heavy for me to hold on.
I'm losing my left self
daily just to keep you alive in me.

-I like to read books much,
but nowadays I love
reading his eyes.
In his untold stories
I'm lost completely.

-You broke the strings of my heart
which use to sing your name
in love, with love

<u>Subrat Pattanaik</u>

-Loving you is easier
Than to forgetting those
Permanent memories
Of yours.

-Every failure night
Experience a successful bright
Where your harkworks fights
For your actual rights!

-I let her go
Out of my sight
Far from my reach
Forever in my life.

-It's hard to get
Someone perfect
In this era of illusion

Shalini Toppo

-The calm amidst the chaos
the stillness even in ripples
the void resting even in cacophony
it is right there; yet not there
the peace; an inner virtue

-At the end of the day you need to hold on to something called
"HOPE"

Your "Hope"
Your Happiness than Other People's Expectations

-Be the good, do the good
be grateful, be generous
what you think is what you are
what you feel is what you are
dictate the right words to let the inner worth bloom

-falling down, will bruise you
falling down, will hurt you
never ever try to 'fall' in love
rather; rise in love, grow in love,
love the love; for the greater good

<u>Prerana Rath</u>

-Judgements now-a-days are as fickle as people's mind.
 Don't let them snatch your dreams and potential.

-Self- pity is the greatest loss you would gift yourself.
 You can't just pity the warrior inside you has survived a lot.

-If it's more pain and less smiles darling it's not your thing .
It's a lesson learn well and move on with gratitude. Universe has much more for you

-I am a whole different person now, I can't contain bit of negative energy, love myself more and moreover see the world through the glasses of kindness no matter what they think of me
That's the power of optimism.

Arshi Ali

-Follow your passion Passionately.

-Every time you challenge me I will commit myself to the task and give you unexpected successful outcomes.

-Our busyness is always a hurdle to give time to each other but even for a minute when we talk feels like relief to the soul.

-Never let your smile reveal your sorrows.

Gritiksha Varma

-Cute:
When she close her eyes for a kiss and his lips touched her forehead

-From running after him for his naughtiness,
To walking after him for taking 'Saptapadi'
Best friends became best couple

-"I hate myself..!!" He snapped

"But I love you and you should love what your love loves..!" She winked

Both smiled and hugged each other!!

-She updated status :
Feeling happy..

The walls of her washroom,
her pillow , her diary and
her dark circles smirked from side!

Aditi Gupta

-The moon whispered, To my ear
Have a nap my dear
For whom you are wasting your tears
That person will not hear.

-What will you do without me?
He asked..
Will feel like a free bird..
I replied

-'Forever' -Just a word of few letters
But have billions of emotions..
It's presence can make you
And absence can break you.

-The day when
You will hold my hand again
And will say you are mine

Short Story

<u>Rhea Ghosh</u>

<u>//Never forget to shine//</u>

Starting a new day is simply like starting something new with hope and faith to succeed, and this is the thought of Radhika Mishra. A girl who just passed CBSE boards exam and now trying to figure out her stream of passion and the best college for her dream to become something bigger and to grow awareness among people about the "do's and don'ts" of thoughts and thinking. Radhika was very much interested in reading and exploring the principles of mind and its working, and hence she is a very bright and cheerful girl but the thing that bothers her is that she never likes to work under anyone rather she always chooses to lead the path.

But one morning when she woke up and got the news that she cleared the state nursing exam which she had given a few days earlier, astonished her. She never wanted nursing as her career but she chose to give this exam along with other exams as this exam has more job opportunities than other exam, but it was a bit saddening news to her that she cracked the nursing exam. Though her parents were very happy by this news and hence she thought of giving this career opportunity a try rejecting the other exams.

With the thought of a new place and new environment Radhika was a hell lot excited and being the only girl child of her parents she was also pampered but not spoiled due to her maturity towards life. Within a few days she shifted to the new college and besides the college building was her hostel and the place was also very warming. From next day onwards her college was going to start and she was very excited for that but when she came face to face with the saddening truth that she will not be able to get out of the college or hostel for any reason and only her parents will be able to visit her on a single Sunday in a month and that she would be caged over there with no possibilities to get out of the hostel gate and also she was not even allowed to visit the canteen without the hostel warden. With this news she cried the whole night but didn't let her parents know as they wanted her to do the course because a job opportunity matters more to a middle class family than dreams and passion but that didn't means that her parents didn't loved her rather they loved her like hell but money matters when you belong to a middle class family background. And hence Radhika decides to focus on the studies which she was good at, but at that point of time her classes was also not yet properly started and hence she was only having the thought to run away from that place, she even planned a hell lot of things like how she would run away if she needed to and what she would do if she ran away and all the different methods that she will try when she would have the chance to.

The next morning she was more like astonished by hearing about the dress code of the college and even a separate dress at the eating place, that every student would be needed to wear proper salwar suit everywhere also no one can ever leave their hair open, and still that was fine to her but here comes another twist her co-ordinator, who was very strict and frustrated for no reason also was very demoralizing and her taunts in every single sentence disturbed her a lot. And all these daily humiliation along with the course of this nursing made Radhika's life tougher and tougher. She knew that she didn't have the choice of leaving this course and hence she tried hard to adjust. But problems never stopped coming and after a few months suddenly one morning Radhika was called by the principal mam of her college and she was accused that she wasn't having any interest in nursing and rather she was motivating her batch mates to leave the course. She was totally shocked with the news as she had no idea about what was principal mam saying, she was scolded a lot by her principal mam and when she came back to her room, she got to know about the conspiracy that her rivals in class had made due to the jealousy that they had against Radhika because of her topping in every subjects without having any interest but she never tried to inspire anyone to leave the course ,and by hearing all these she now had only one single thought in her mind and that was to run away and never come back but she loved her parents to much to hurt them like this. Thinking about all these humiliation, the course of nursing, taunts of the coordinator and along with all these she also started to have a few disputes with her parents, now at this situation all these things led her to only one thought in mind and that was "to run away". And something very surprising happened that night which led her to run away that day itself, and that she was accused of manipulating some official records, and she was suspended from college for a month and also her parents were called and her parents denied to accept the truth that she haven't done anything, now nothing was left for her to stay over here and that night itself she planned to run away. When everyone slept that night she took her luggage bag and backpack and silently took the keys from the warden mams room and left with leaving a note over her bed that "I'm leaving this course and I haven't done any of the thing I'm blamed for." After that she hurriedly jumped from the fence with her luggage and ran for the nearest station then she took the train to Howrah in West Bengal and then she changed her clothes in the station washroom to have less chances for identification and from there she took a train to Mumbai, after she reached Mumbai she called her mom and dad from a shop after three days from she left hostel. She cried a lot and then picked up her courage and said her parents that she is gonna be perfectly fine and that she will return home after five years and then she disconnected the call. Her mom dad tried every possible way to find her but till then she has reached beyond the reach of her mom dad. Police also tried hard to trace her but she was unreachable, she stayed in an Ashram, practiced meditation daily to make herself stronger, joined a nearby psychology college and is now pursuing her degree from there, and studying from library books, she travels a long distance only to call her parents once a month and to avoid any identification if her parents tried to reach her.

After three years she graduated from that college by topping the course with the best marks and along with that she works as a counsellor at the ashram and is now applying for a Masters in psychology. Now the ashram has become her family and she lives peacefully over there and enjoy parting knowledge. She is now in a state where all her dreams are coming true one by one. Her parents tried a lot to find her but they lost their hope and hence they were satisfied with the random calls Radhika made once in a month.

After a few years Radhika came back home with the degree and a reputed job in her hand along with her research work, her parents were overjoyed with her homecoming and her life became happier. Now whatever asks from her parents they never denied that and even now her parents respected her decisions. Only one big step in Radhika's life made heaven, now she is a scientist and is working happily on her dreams.

Nothing is bigger than our passion and dream, and the only thing a person needs to have enough courage to make their life happy. And as usual the best thing comes out in the worst situations. But still no matter what never forget to shine.

उक्तियाँ / शायरी

Neha Khatri

-कुछ तेरी रूह पर अधूरे अल्फ़ाज़ लिखे हुए है,कुछ मेरी रूह पर ,
उससे रब ने मिलाया हम दोनों को एक गज़ब शायरी लिखने के लिए।

-उसके ज़ख़्मों को चूमकर ऐसे अपना बनाया मैंने,
जैसे मंदिर के आगे उस भगवान के सामने माथा टेक कर अपना माना
मैंने।

-बटुए में रूपए भले ही कितने भी हो
शौक पहले मेरे पुरे करके ही
खुश मेरी माँ हो लेती है
अपने ख़्वाबों की तिजोरी पर ताला लगाए बैठी
मेरी मंज़िल की दुआ वो हमेशा करती है।

-इन जिस्मों के बाज़ार में उसने मेरी रूह को खरीद लिया
अंधेरों के जहाँ में वो रौशनी बनकर मुझे मिल गया।

Ayush Vaidya

-अगर उससे तुम मिलो तो ये ज़रूर पूछना कि तुम कैसी हो,

इस जालिम दुनिया में तुम उसके हो चाहे वो जैसी भी हो।

-लगता है अभी अभी तुमने पलकें झपकाई और रात हो गई,

फिर तुमने आँख बंद किया और मैं सो गया।

-ए ख़ुदा! कैसी ये तेरी मर्ज़ी है, सुनता नहीं तू सबकी अर्जी है,

सब करते तुमसे फरमाइश, होती पुरी किसी-किसी ख़्वाहिश,

मेरी भी माँगे कर दे पूरी, कसम से! नहीं बनाऊँगा तुमसे दूरी ।

-यूँ न रूख जान-ए-मन, एक बार देख ले कर के इकरार,

मुझे पता है तू भी है बेक़रार ,

और लगता है तुम कर रही हो इंतजार कि फिर आ के मना ले रूठे हुए

को एक बार।

<u>Amol Mishra</u>

-लापरवाह उसकी मोहब्बत

बेपनाह बर्बाद हुए हम,

तवज़्ज़ो दिया उन्होंने किसी और को

खामखाँ बदनाम हुए हम..

-क्या मिला तुम्हें हमें बर्बाद करके,

एक हँसी रहती थी होंठों पर वो भी छीन ली।

-दुख दर्द सब ज़िंदगी का हिस्सा है,

तू मेरे लिए अब एक बीता हुआ किस्सा है।

-मेरी नसों में तेरे नाम का ज़हर भर दिया...

मोहब्बत तो मुझसे की फिर खुद को किसी और का क्यों कर दिया।

Akash Nandy

-उनके किरदार की चर्चा कहाँ होती है ।।

बस उस तद्रीस की सदा आती हैं ।।

तुम समेट लो उनके आशीर्वाद और उसूलों को ।।

बिना गुरु के ज़िंदगी कहाँ चल पाती है ।।

-मैं साहिल हूँ, बेशुमार शराब रखता हूँ ।

बस एक तेरे आँखों के समुद्र में समा जाना चाहता हूँ ।।

मैं खुद छलकता जाम हूँ हर महफ़िलों का ।

तेरे होठों का जाम पीकर तेरे नाम से मशहूर होना चाहता हूँ ।।

-ये आँसू उनके दिया हुआ तोहफ़ा है, तो चलो आजइन्हें बहा लेते हैं ।।

मेरे दिल के दर्द को देखना चाहते हो तो चलो,

आज हम और तुम मिलकर शराब पी लेते हैं ।।

-तेरे दिल के कफ़स में अब मेरी याद नहीं ।

अब अपनी यादों से कह दो तेरे नैनों का जाम मेरे होंठों पे छलकाए नहीं

।।

तू साथ नहीं है तो ज़िंदगी के रंज-ओ-गम से भी कोई शिकवे नहीं हैं ।

जा चली जा अब मुझे तेरे जाने का कोई गम नहीं है ।।

Niharika

-पहली मुलाकात में दिया तेरा वह फूल आज भी सहेज के रखा है मैंने,

कि जब तुम मिलो तो तुम्हें बताएं कितनी मोहब्बत है तुमसे।

-ठंडी हवाओं का झोंका,
कानों में कुछ कह गया।

याद उसकी आई,
कमबख्त दिल फिर पिघल गया।

-देख कर तुझे ये हुस्न,
और निखर जाता है।
शर्मा जाती हूं मैं,
और यह दिल मचल जाता है।

लोग कहते हैं,
कि तुझे प्यार हो गया है।
सच मानो तो दिल का,
बुरा हाल हो गया है।

Hrittish Singh

-मैं तो आशिक़ हूँ जनाब,

बस किस्से-कहानियों में सिमट जाना चाहता हूँ।

ख्वाहिश भी नही कोई फूलों जैसी,

बस कलम की निब से लिपट जाना चाहता हूँ।

-लोगों से ही जीने का ये हुनर सीख रहा हूँ,

खुद को ही पढ़ता हूँ अब खुद को ही लिख रहा हूँ।

-बेवज़ह और बेवक्त तो मैं खूब ठहाके लगाता हूँ,

हर वक्त मुस्कुराने की वजह ढूँढ रहा हूँ।

-मोहब्बत कम नहींहुई...

बस, हमारे बीच की थोड़ी जगह हमारी मजबूरियों ने किराए पर ले रखी

है!

Ansh Manoj Mishra

-रिश्ते को आगे बढ़ाने का उनका भी इरादा था, प्यार बरकरार रखने का उनका भी वादा था,

एकतरफ़ा नहीं,इश्क़ उनकी तरफ से भी जागा था, वैसे तो बेहद चाहती थी वो हमें,

पर इश्क़ हमें कुछ ज्यादा था।

पर इश्क़ हमें कुछ ज्यादा था।।

-हां,हमारी ज्यादा बात नही होती,

एक दूसरे की बाहों में फिलहाल रात नहीं होती, तो क्या हुआ??

तो क्या हुआ,जो दोनों में अभी थोड़ी दूरी है,

थोड़ा इंतजार रखिए दास्तां इश्क़ की अभी अधूरी है।।

-मै लफ्ज़ हूं,

मेरी बात तुम हो...

मै तब हूं,

जब मेरे साथ तुम हो...

-तेरे नैनोंमें मदहोश ये शाम हो,

मेरे लब तेरे लबों के गुलाम हो।।

Aryan Arora

-खुशियों के सफर परहूँ गम का आशियाना नहीं चाहिए,

तू मिलातो मिली जीने की वजह अब मरने का बहाना नही चाहिए।

-उसको देखा तो आँखे झुक गई,

खुली हवा में सांसे रुक गयी।

-कौन कहता है कि मैं तुझसे जुदा हूँ,

लोग देख नही पाते क्योंकि तेरी रूह से जुड़ा हूँ।

-कई बातें मेरे दिल में रहती हैं,

नहीं सुनता मैं जो मुझसे मेरी दिल की धड़कने कहती हैं,

और जब चाह कर भी किसी को बोल नही पाता ,

तब आंखों से आँसू और कलम से सियाही बहती है।

Om Rajesh Gupta

-उससे मोहब्बत करते होगे तो उसे दिल से देखोगे,

इस दुनिया मे आंखों से तो बस घूरा जाता है।

प्यार करना है तो शिद्दत से करो ना,

जुनून वाला प्यार तो उसको तुम्हारे न होने से खत्म हो जाता है।

-रात के सन्नाटों का शोर गूंज रहा है ऐसे,

मेरे प्यार को अनदेखा कर दिया था तुमने जैसे।

दूसरो के नज़रिए से अब देखने लगा हूँ,

चल दिया हूँ एक तरफ़ा आशिक़ के जैसे।

-ज़िन्दगी कुछ इस क़दर हसीन हो गयी है,

हम दोस्ती करने गए थ और क्या बताऊँ मोहब्बत सी हो गई है।

-हम कलसे काफी ख़फा रहते हैं इसलिये शायद आज भी उदास बैठे हैं,

बाहर तो निकल उस ज़ख्म से,

सुना है यहांपर छोटे छोटे के भी इतिहास बड़े गहरे है।

<u>*Ayushka*</u>

-तेरी तस्वीर से मोहब्बत को पाल रखा है,

अपनी नींद से तेरा ख्वाब निकाल रखा है,

ज़िन्दगी का हर लम्हा खो दिया मैंने,

पर तेरी यादों को अभी तक संभाल रखा है।

-तेरी ज़ज़्बातों पे लिखी किताब हूँ मैं,

तेरी शायरी तेरी ग़ज़ल तेरा ख्वाब हूँ मैं,

एक दफा तो देख खोल कर,

तेरी रूह का प्यार हूँ मैं।

-तुझे खुद में बसने की चाहत ने,

हमे खुद से ही जुदा कर दिया,

क्या खेल रचाया किस्मत ने,

कातिल को ही खुदा कर दिया।

-गुमनाम है वो दिया

जिसकी रोशनी में हम जलते थे,

अब तो अंधेरा ही छाया रहता है

सिर्फ गुमनाम से दिल जलते है।

Poorvi Kumar

-खो दिया मैंने उसे जिसे दिल से मैंने माँगा था,

ना जाने अब किस मोड़ पे आ कर हमारा अफसाना था,

कुछ पल थे शायद हाथ में हमारे,

पर उसकी जुबां पे तो किसी और के प्यार का नज़राना था।

-इश्क़ वो नहीं जो लफ़्ज़ों में बयां हो जाए,

आँखों ही आँखों में हाल -ए -दिल बयां हो जाए,

ये वो एहसास है जो उसके सामने आते ही आपकी नज़र झुक जाए।

-इतने रंग मत दिखाना ऐ ज़िंदगी तू मुझे,

कहीं मैं मुस्कुराना ना भूल जाऊँ,

यूँ तो अकेले सजाया था मैंने,

तेरे दिए हर रंग को,

इतने रंग मत दिखाना तू मुझे

कहीं मैं दर्द से उलझना ना भूल जाऊँ।

-प्यार था आँखों में उसकी,

अश्कों में झलकती थी फ़िक्र उसकी,

ये अफसाना था सच्ची मोहब्बत का,

जो दूर होके भी हीर रांझा जैसी,

कहाँ थी उनकी।

Pranav Bakshi

-मेरे लफ्ज़ की गहराई में,
छुपी उसकी तनहाई है।

जिससे सदियों पहले का रिश्ता टूट गया था,
वो आज भी दिल में समाई हैं।

-ख्वाबों की नुमाइश थी,
कीमत तो चुकानी थी।

उसको पाने की गुज़ारिश थी,
आखिर जान तो गँवानी थी।

-एक ऐसा एहसास हो तुम,
ना जाने कैसा ख्वाब हो तुम।

जैसा भी राज़ हो तुम,
दिल के बहुत खास हो तुम।

-कश्मकश में फंसे,
मेरे ये जज़्बातहैं,

कह भी ना पाऊं,
ऐसे ये हालात हैं।

Aanya Mithal

-आपसे मोहब्बत सज़ा हो गयी....

रात की नींद, दिन का चैन था बस...

वो भी हमसे छीन ले गयी...

-तुमसे मोहब्बत है,

नहीं चाहिए बताने को कलम की सियाही...

तुमसे जुदाई मंज़ूर नहीं है,

तो हम भी लिखने लगे शेर-ओ-शायरी।

-तुम्हें समझते समझते थक गई हूँ...

तुम्हें समझते समझते तक गयी हूँ...

ऐ खुदा मेरी गलती बता दे मुझे,

मैं खुद को भूल चली हूँ....

-तुम्हारे नाम में ही सच था....

हमारी तो ज़िन्दगी ही झूठ की नींव पर थी...

तुम्हारे आने से क्या बदलाव लाये...

बेगाने हम, चोकाने हमारे यार रह गए।

Sinchita

-आज वो कशिश न थी,
फिर तेरी बातों में,
कुछ मौसम में नमी थी,
कुछ तेरी आँखों में।

-यह ज़रूरी नहीं,
खुशी हमेशा अंदर से आए,
चाँद भी तो,
किसी और की रौशनी में चमकता है।

-कई बार खुद को समझाया,
कि वो एहसास कहीं गुम थे,
यह नज़रों का है धोखा,
या फिर वो सचमें तुम थे।

-मेरे सिरहाने में रखा एक किताब,
फटे पन्नों में छिपा एक गुलाब,
उन दिनों की याद दिलाता है,
जब मिलना हमारी ज़रूरत नहीं, आदत थी।

कविताएँ

Tatsat Pandey

///दो धड़कने///

अरे सुनो, थोड़ी देर रुक जाओ

कुछ पल और ठहर जाओ,

ये बोल कर,वह उसे रोकता है

कुछ मीठे, कुछ चुलबुली बातें

और किये जाओ,

ये बोल कर, वह उसे समझाता है,

बात उन दोनों की कुछ निराली है

पाँच मिनट दे कर भी उनके

रिश्ते में खुशहाली है।

अल्फ़ाज़ नहीं है,अंदाज़ नहीं है

ये उस रिश्ते की कहानी है,

कुछ प्यारी कुछ न्यारी

ये दो धड़खनो की बेज़ुबानी है।।

BibiAyeesha Mulla

//*जा तुझे माफ़ किया*//

जा तुझे माफ़ किया

आज हार कर भी जीत से गए हैं हम

तुम्हारे धोके से आज़ाद हुवे हैं हम

तुमने दोस्ती महज़ एक मतलब के लिए की थी

मतलब ख़तम होने पर जान पाए हैं हम

कभी सोचा ना था इस मुक़ाम पर होंगे हम

जहाँ इंतेखाब करना होगा तुम्हे किसी और को

शिकायत करूँ भी किस से जो अपना ना रहा

माफ़ी तो मांग ली तुमने दुखा कर दिल हमारा

हम ने माफ़ भी कर दिया जब वो गैर भी हुआ

शिकवे तो अपनों से होते हैं जो वो अब ना रहा

Shashwat Trivedi

//ज़िंदगी से ज़िंदगी के लिए//

ज़िन्दगी से ज़िन्दगी के लिए, कुछ मैं भी प्यार मांग लूं,

एक खुशियों की दास्तान लिखनी है, कुछ शब्द उधार मांग लूं,

शायद फिर कभी तुम्हें, भरोसा रहे या ना रहे,

कुछ लम्हों के लिए तुमसे, तुम्हारा ऐतबार मांग लूं।

हमने भी ग़म के सहारे, ज़िन्दगी बिता दी बहुत,

अब खुदा से दुआ में अपनी, मैं खुशियां हज़ार मांग लूं,

तेरी पलकें भीगें नही, कभी हार जाने के डर से,

मैं रब से तेरी जीत मांगकर, अपने हिस्से में हार मांग लूं।

Soumya Swarup Nayak

//खिलौना तो टूटा है एक//

खिलौना तो टूटा है एक

आवाज़ तो नहीं हुई टूटने की मगर

चीख जरूर निकली होंगी

सिसक भी जगी होगी

बार -बार, हर बार, जब उसे तोड़ा गया होगा

मरोड़ा गया होगा

परत दर परत, हिस्सा दर हिस्सा।

यूँ एक गुड़िया सी सुन्दर रही होगी वोनन्ही जान

जिसे गुड़िया-से रंग बिरंगी कपड़े पहना कर भेजती होगी उसकी माँ मेले
में

या यूनिफार्म पहनाकर स्कूल

जहाँ पढ़ा होगा उसने इंसानियत का बड़ा बड़ा पाठ

बिलकुल उसके उलट जो उसने महसूस किया होगा उस पल

जब आँखों के आंसुओ से आत्मा को उसके छेद दीया गया होगा उसके

उन दरिंदो के द्वारा

जब अंग दर अंग खुदा की इस बंदी को जलील कियागया होगा

उसके अहम् को बिखेरा गया होगा

जिससे खिलौने की तरह खेला गया आज।

माफ़ करना इंसानियत पर तेरे बाजार में

झूठी शान इंसानियत से थोड़ी महंगी बिक गयी आज शायद

समझ में भी जंग लगी शायद

वरना वो तनया खिलौने सी नाजुक तो थी

पर खिलौना नहीं थी

जिससे तुम यूँ खेल गए।

<u>Vivek Kumar Shaw</u>

<u>//किरदार//</u>

डाल कर पर्दा अपने किरदार पर

हर शख़्स कह रहा जमाना खराब है।

कहानियाँ तो सही लिखता है ईश्वर

खराबियां तो अपने किरदारों में जनाब है।

एक छत के नीचे असत्य की दीवार है,

मानो हर तरफ झूठ का बाजार है,

एक दूसरेसे मिलना भी जिसमे दुश्वार है,

जिसके किस्से का हर कोई अलग अलग किरदार है।

ठोकर खाये इंसान के ईमान नही पिघलते हैं,

कुछ किरदारों से वफादारी के आंसू निकलते हैं।

कुछ किरदारों में खामियां नजर आतीहैं,

रात के अंधेरों में वे हैवान बन जाते हैं।

शब्द सब वही हैं कुछ विचार अपने लाये,

कवियों की बस्ती में ढंग सीखने आये हैं।

कुछ लोगो के किरदार मैंने

अपने डायरी में रचे हैं,

वे शख्स जिसे पढ़ खूब हंसे है।

हवा के रुख देख वे अपने किरदार बदलतेहैं,
सियासत की साजिशों में वे अपना ईमान बदले हैं।

अच्छा है या बुरा है, समय बीत जाएगा
मिलाकर मिट्टी में चालबाजों को मेरी कविता जीत जाएगी।
मुख से अगर झूठ की चट्टाने गिरी, विवाद
सारे और बढ़ जाएंगे,
सम्मान अगर दुनिया से मिटा, तो रिश्ते सारे जल जाएंगे।
है अगर मेरी सच्ची कथन, अगर सच्चे मेरे गीत हैं
हार जाएंगे सोच अपराधियो के,यही हमारी जीत है।

Apoorva Suryavanshi

//तुम्हारी आंखें//

पास बैठ जब तुम वो तरह तरह से मुझे चिढ़ाते हो,

फिर कभी चुप होकर बस टक-टक ताके जाते हो,

वो जब शर्म से झुका मेरा चेहरा उठाते हो,

उसी पल लगता है मानो

शराबी शराबी तुम्हारी आंखे,

बड़ी चंचल तुम्हारी आंखें,

दीवानी दीवानी तुम्हारी आंखें ,

मेरे आप कहने पर

कव्वाली कव्वाली तुम्हारी आंखें,

हवा से झुकी तुम्हारी आंखे,

मतवाली मतवाली तुम्हारी आंखें।

पाक दामन तुम्हारी आंखे,

मेरे घर का आंगन तुम्हारी आंखे,

मक्का मदीना तुम्हारी आंखें,

चारो धाम तुम्हारी आंखें,

मूक अभिव्यक्ति तुम्हारी आंखें,

पढ़ लो तो गीता कुरान तुम्हारी आंखें।

समझ लो तो सागर से गहरी तुम्हारी आंखें,

गंगा से पवित्र तुम्हारी आंखें,

बच्चो की अबोध मुस्कान तुम्हारी आंखे,

बड़ी महम है प्रियतम तुम्हारी आंखें।

Shreyashi Shrivastav

//इश्क पुराना नहीं होता//

पहली सहर से रंगीन शाम तक,

खिलते आफताब से ढलते महताब तक,

वो मेरी हर बात में याद बेशुमार रहता है,

उसके इश्क का मुझे एक अलग ही खूमार रहता है,

मैं सितारे नहीं ला सकती वरना आसमान सूना पड़ जाता,

तुम मिल गए तो सूकून की नींद आ गई वरना हर ख्वाब अधूरा रह

जाता,

कभी फुरसत में बैठूंगी तो सब बताऊंगी,

दिल के इस किताब का हर पन्ना पढ़ कर सुनाऊंगी,

अक्स जिसे कहते हैं ना बस वही बन गए हो,

मौत से डर नहीं तुम जिंदगी बन गए हो,

आज भी तुम हकीकत बनते हो ना तो हर ख्वाब नूराना हो जाता है,

कौन कहता है इश्क पुराना हो जाता है...

Shreyansh Gupta

//तुम लौट कर आओगी जरूर//

हाँ तेरी यादों ने मुझे बेख्याली में भुलाया है,

हाँतेरी बातों ने मुझे बेरहमी से सताया है,

हाँतूने मेरे दिल को बेदर्दी से तड़पाया है,

हाँतूने इन अश्कों को बेपनाह रुलाया है,

हाँ तुझ पर बेवफाई का लगा हर इल्जाम है मुझपे मंजूर

फिर भी, दिल कहता है तुम लौट कर आओगी जरूर...

जब साथ मांगा तुम्हारा तो राह मोड़ गई तुम...

जब दिल दिया तुम्हे तो उसे तोड़ गई तुम...

जब हाथ दिया तुम्हे तो उसे छोड़ गई तुम...

नाम मोहब्बत बताया और चादर बेवफाई का ओढ़ गई तुम??

लगाएहैं तुम पर दर्द-ए-गुनाह के लाख मैंने कसूर...

फिर भी दिल कहता है तुम लौट कर आओगी जरूर...

याद है जब मेरी बाहों में गुजरती थी तेरी रातें

और सुबह तक करते थे हम एक दूसरे से बातें

एक तरफ हो गई वो बातें एक तरफ हो गया प्यार मेरा...

बस रह गई तेरी यादें और वो झूठा ऐतबार तेरा...

यूँ तो इस एक तरफा रिश्ते पर भी है मुझे गुरुर

फिर भी दिल कहता है तुम लौट कर आओगी जरूर...

टूट कर टुकड़ों में ख्वाहिशें मेरी बिखर गई..

समेटा इन्हें अल्फाजों में और आवाज इनकी निखर गई..

ये कैसी तेरी चाहत... ये कैसा मेरा प्यार...

तुम आओगी नहीं और मैं करता रहूंगा इंतजार..

अमावस की रात चांद तलाशने सा छाया है मुझ पर फितूर..

क्योंकि दिल कहता है तुम लौट कर आओगी जरूर...

खामोशियों के शोर में आवाज़ तेरी आती है...

तनहाईयों की करवटों में आवाज़ तेरी आती है...

सोचता हूं तुझे तो यही बात ज़ेहन में आती है..

तु दूर है मुझसे फिर भी तु दूर क्यों नहीं जाती है..

तेरी यादों के नशें में हैं अल्फाज मेरे चूर

क्योंकि दिल कहता है तुम लौट कर आओगी जरूर...

मैं गुम हो गया हूं कहीं तेरी तलाश में...

बेसब्र हो रहा है दिल तेरे आने की आस में...

नफ़रत सी अब होने लगी है मुझे इस इंतजार से

नफ़रत सी अब होने लगी है मुझे अपने ही प्यार से

इतनी नफ़रतो में भी मोहब्बत करने को हूँमजबूर

क्योंकि दिल कहता है तुम लौट कर आओगी जरूर...

Vanshdeep Singh

///शायर//

ना कभी छोड़ना साथ मेरा

यह रोज़ मैं कहना चाहता हूँ,

है तुमसे कितना प्यार मुझे

ये कभी नहीं कह पाता हूँ।

सब बातें सबसे कह देता

तुझसे कहने से कतराता हूँ,

कहीं गुस्से में छोड़ ना चली जाओ

यह सोच के मैं डर जाता हूँ।

वैसे तो नहीं डरता हूँ मैं

तुझे खोने के ख्याल ने कायर बनाया है,

तेरी आंखों ने घायल किया मुझे

तेरी यारी ने शायर बनाया है।

Subiya Sayeda

//एक मोहब्बत ऐसी भी//

हां! वो मेरे साथ ही कालेज में पढ़ती थी।

बेशक हमारी रोज मुलाकात होती थी,

पर कहां कोई मुकम्मल सी बात होती थी।

जिसे देख लफ्ज़ पिंजरे में छिप जाते थे,

कहना तो बहुत कुछ था पर कहाँ ये साथ निभाते थे ।

वो दिल में ग़म-ओ-जहां का कर्ज़ उठाती थी,

शबनमी आंखों में कहकशां-सा समाती थी ।

जिसके अहसास भर से गुल खिल जाते थे,

तितलियां मुस्कान से रंग चुराती थीं ।

पलकें झपकने से इंकार करतीं,

निगाहें पलटने से तकरार करतीं ।

शर्म-ओ-हया कि वो मूरत,

जन्नत की हूरों से भी खुबसूरत ।

आफताब जिसे देख बादलों में गोते लगाता,

मेहताब जिसके आते ही शफाक हो जाता।

मुसलसल खामोशी इख़्तेयार किये हुए,

वो चलती थी शमां की आह लिए हुए ।

तिरंछी नजरों से मैं उसे देख रहा था,

पर उसके आते ही दिशाओं का रूख बदला करता था ।

बातें ढेर सारी आईने को सुनाता था,
पर उसके आते ही मानो मुझे सांप सूंघ जाता था।

वक्त की रफ्तार के साथ सब बदल गया
मैं भी,
वो भी,
वो दौर भी....
पर,
आज भी कभी कभी उसकी यादें,
रात के अंधेरे में चुपके से,
मेरे दरवाजे पर दस्तक देती है ।
उससे ना सही, उसके अक्स से मेरी बातें होती हैं ।

मैं उससे कहता हूँ,
कि आज भी उसके हिस्से का वक्त
मैं उसी कि याद में गुज़ारता हूँ ।
उन्हीं गलियों में उसे तलाशता हूँ ,
उन्हीं बादलों में उसे तराशता हूँ ।
आज भी आसमां का कोई तारा टूटे
तो मैं उसकी हिफाज़त की दुआएं मांगता हूँ ।

वो,
मेरी मिल्कियत ना सही,
मेरी मोहब्बत है ।

वो,
मेरा खुदा तो नहीं,
मेरी इबादत है ।

उसकी यादें तनहाईयों को मिटा कर
मेरे साथ चाय की चुस्कीयां लेती हैं ।
उन दिनों की बातें होती है,
ऐसे ना जाने कितनी शामों की सुबहें होती हैं।

Neha Mahavir Lunkad

//अधूरी ख्वाहिश//

तुम मेरे पास न सही,

तेरा जिक्र आज भी है!

मेरे चेहरे पे नफरत सही,

दिल में चाहत आज भी है!

तेरा साथ आज नहीं,

यादें दफन आज भी है!

प्यार मेरा पूरा न हो सका,

आस पूरा करने की आज भी है!

तुझे, खो दिया था मैंने कल,

मिलने की ख्वाहिश आज भी है!

कुछ अधूरा था प्यार का सिलसिला,

मुकम्मल हो प्यार, तमन्ना आज भी है!

//वक्त//

वक्त रहते वक्त ने बताया,

कौन है अपना और कौन पराया,

कहीं खो गई थी पराये लोगो में,

वक्त ने अब है मुझे समझाया,

अपनो को छोड़ दिया था कहीं,

खो गई थी गैरों की दुनिया में,

अब आया है समझ गैरों में रह कर,

गलत थी मैं जो छोड़ गई अपनो को गैरों में।

Co-authors

Aayushi Gupta

My name is Aayushi Gupta, a student of BA (Hons.) English, from Jaipur. My contact numbers are 8441992220 and 7043581745. My email Id is <u>aayushig1907@gmail.com</u>.

Aanya Mithal

My name is Aanya Mittal.
I am from Delhi , currently i live in jaipur for my secondary education with my Granny.
I am preparing for iit , i am in 11th.
I don't own a personal phone , its my interest or eagerness I manage using instagram on my Grannie's phone.

Aditi Gupta

Aditi Gupta from Haridwar, Uttarakhand. Pursuing graduation in biotechnology from Dehradun. A passionate rifle shooter. And a writer who loves to be lost while writing

Akash Nandy

Myself Akash Nandy. Electrical Engineer by profession and a writer by passion. Recently working with Jindal groups Ltd in nashik as a textile engineer.

<u>Aritra Kundu</u>

Aritra kundu , from navi mumbai an MBBS graduate writing to soothe the ears and eyes of the world through my words.

<u>Ansh Manoj Mishra</u>

Name:Ansh Manoj Mishra
City:Mumbai
Education: studying in 10th standard

<u>Amol Mishra</u>

I'm Amol Mishra Admin of @noise.of.heart
I'm from Hardoi UP
It's the Noise Of my heart which i wrote

<u>Apoorva Suryavanshi</u>

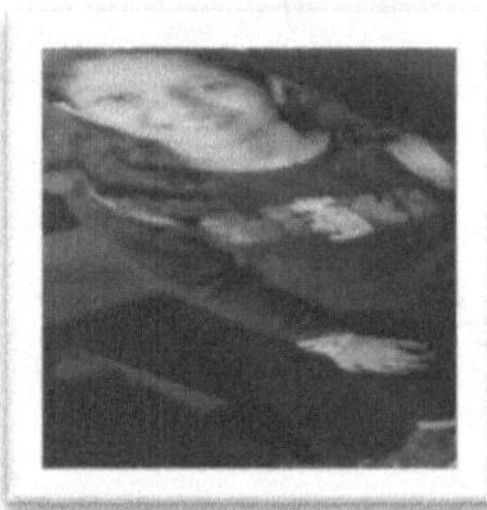

I am Apoorva Suryavanshi from Basti , Uttar Pradesh. I am in class 10 in St.Basil's School,Basti . I love to write about 90z love rather than teenage love . Lots of love. Keep reading !

<u>Arihana Saikia</u>

This is Arihana Saikia and I am a 13 year old girl living in Mumbai. I started writing 3 years ago and it's been a great journey till now. I drop down my feelings in a piece of paper and post it on Instagram

<u>Arshi Ali</u>

An Introvert person student of Jagran Lakecity University, Bhopal.
Pursuing law and has been writing since 2012. Published author of the book Reflected Souls.

<u>Aryan Arora</u>

I am Aryan Arora S/O Mr Atul Arora And Mrs Neetu Arora.I am a student of class 12th studying in St.basil's school, Basti Uttar Pradesh.I am writing from last 4 years and I want to achieve something great in this field

<u>Ayushka</u>

Ayushka Pandey
Class 10 at St Basil's School Basti
Love is writing
Enjoying life in self company

Ayush Vaidya

Ayush Vaidya
Patna, Bihar
Studying in BCA 2nd year
Loves to write. A Joyful Soul who never forgets to smile and make others smile.

Banasmita Bahera

My heart beats for farmers and my pen runs in the thought of reality..An Agricultural Engineer by profession and a writer by passion.This is dedicated to my family.... Love u all and happy reading

BibiAyeesha Mulla

Name: Bibiayeesha Mulla
Education : Dental student 3rd yr

Gritiksha Varma

I'm Gritiksha Varma from Gujarat,
Studying BHMS
Dr. (Future) by occupation,
Writer by passion

<u>Charu Sharma</u>

Charu Sharma , She is a college student currently pursuing Bachelor in Journalism and Mass communication. She is a small town girl with not so small dreams . Her genre of writing consists of one liners , poems , shayari , stories , articles and quotes. Her hobbies are singing and dancing . She wanna take writing as a profession and not just her passion . She is a soft hearted girl and loves to explore new things , she is a passionate soul . You can see the love in her eyes and fire in her soul. She totally believes the mantra that a pen is mightier than the sword . She wants her readers to relate to the content she makes. She wants to spread happiness and positivity. She motivates people to make Earth a better place to live in. She sees beauty in everything she sees. Trust her and you can explore yourself better.
You can follow her on Instagram
@herheartjourney

<u>Hrittish Singh</u>

I am a family oriented person. Working as a freelance writer by profession. I am a country boy with a simple lifestyle. I am a happy go lucky kind of a person who dreams big and also thrives hard to fulfill them.

<u>Isha Singhal</u>

I'm Isha Singhal from haridwar city.
I'm pursuing my graduation in microbiology.
My mail Id - ishasinghal849@gmail.com

Karthika Padmakumar

My name's Karthika and I come from the God's own Country! I'm a literature Student and you can catch me on instagram and wordpress.

Kshama Rao

Kshama Rao is the author of several books. Recently she received the Literoma achiever's award for her work as an author.

Lakshita Shrimali

An escapist from Worldly problems seeking solace in Harry Potter, Poems and Pizza!
Lakshita Shrimali a girl of class 11
born and brought up in Udaipur

Mamta Bhagat

A Little Girl I was,
When they Handed me a Pen
To write for every Flaws
Which happens now and then.
Hi, This Is Mamta Bhagat ! I am a Student of Class 11th And I was Brought up In Delhi.

Mehnaaz Shaik

Mehnaaz shaik
Kurnool,Andhra Pradesh
12th passed out
Email- mehnaazshaik2k@gmail.com

Mohammed Ahmed

Mohammed Ahmed resides in United Kingdom, I am an Accounting graduate and also a poet. Ahmed's poetry is melancholic and raw derived from his experience, thoughts and creative mind. He has previously published his personal poetry collection titled 'The Despairationist' and has been a contributing author to many other anthologies.

Mohammed Umar M

I'm Mohammed Umar M from city of Bangalore I have done by B.E Im a chef as well. You can get in touch with me @poetry_maker

Manha Siddique

I am Manha Siddiqui,a 13year old born and brought up in Aligarh. I'm an ardent reader , a bibliophile,a passionate poet , and I love to sketch .

Neha Khatri

I am Neha khatri, i am from a small town bikaner which is situated in rajasthan. I love writing and want to write my own book one day and i believe everything happens when you believe in yourself, just trust the timings of god and keep believing in magic.
You can follow my page
Kuch_ankahi_baatey on Instagram.

Neha Mahavir Lunkad

My Name Is Neha Mahavir Lunkad From Maharashtra.I'm Pursuing Computer Engineering In Last Year Currently,From SNJB's KBJ COE,Chandwad,423101

Niharika Ramteke

I am Niharika Ramteke. A BBA graduate and presently pursuing MBA in marketing. I am passionate poet writer, I love to travel. My home town is
Dalli-Rajhara, Chhattisgarh

Om Rajesh Gupta

Om Rajesh Gupta
Bcom and CA Student
An occasional Writer.

Prerana Rath

I am Prerana Rath . I am an engineering student and a writer by choice. I love playing and experimenting with literature. Words capture my emotions and present them beautifully. My writings are generally of motivating, inspiring and romantic genres.

Priyambada Bahera

My name and my character goes hand in hand. Love to cook,write ,sing and play with Colours

Pranav Bakshi

*Hey I am Pranav Bakshi.I am from a small City 'Basti'.
I am in class 12th. You can contact me -
bakhshipranav56@gmail.com*

Poorvi Kumar

*It's Poorvi Kumar from Basti.
A student of St.Basil's School.
Phn no : 9305191011*

Rhea Ghosh

Me being a Bengali girl,loves to eat sweets a lot and my hobbies are dancing and writing along with reading novels too.

Shreyansh Gupta

Shreyansh Gupta resides in Kolkata and is an 18 yr old microbiology student. His poems are mostly based on Love and Heartbreak and are well published on his Instagram page @_juzz_baat_ . He started writing a yr ago to give a voice to the words stuck inside him. He dreams to find Old School Love in this modern day society and aspires to write his own book soon.

Sinchita

My name is Sinchita and I am currently residing in Greater Noida. I am a Delhi University graduate in History (hons.). I am a hopeless romantic, eccentric, witty and a thinker with a soul of a gypsy.

Simran Arora

A 21 year old girl lost in her whole world. Her destiny has lead her in a dental college. Born on 9th december 1998 in a city, Bahraich(UP), to Mr Anoop kumar Arora and Mrs Anju Arora. Eyes that dream high and a smile that speaks more than words. Owns a pot of memories and a stack of untold Stories that would stir up rage. Lives with fire in her heart and utter chaos in her brain. Have a lot to change in world starting from herself first. A lot to achieve, still have her share of dreams to snatch from her destiny.

Shreyashi Shrivastav

Name-Shreyashi Srivastava
Student of diploma electrical engineering from MMIT siddharth nagar
City-Basti (Uttar Pradesh)
Phone number-7379986767

Subrat Pattanaik

Subrat Pattanaik.. It's me.. From city of temples bhubaneswar... Hello from then fellow final year engineering student..
If anyone ever wants to contact me, mail me in this: subratpattanaik20@gmail.com

Shalini Toppo

**Shalini Toppo, goes by the pen name Shaes
Resides in Raipur
An MBBS graduate
Can find and ping at shaessays@gmail.com**

Shashwat Trivedi

Shashwat Trivedi, the names simply means universal. So, don't know if they'll be universal but just trying to write the things which may last for so long. Which may be relatable for a longer period and they find a mirror image of themselves in the words. Currently a Bachelor's student. Living in Delhi NCR

Subiya Sayeda

*I am Sayeda Subiya battling with words in my early 20's. I am a final year mbbs student, reluctant
not to let the ink in my pen dry.
I strongly believe our work defines us and thats how we would live even after departing .After all,we are all breaths entangled in bodies wishing to leave a mark.*

Shraddha Cholera

*I am shraddha cholera, I am from Rajkot (Gujarat), I am 21 years old MBA student, I love to write my feelings because sometimes it's difficult to speak out publicly, I have only one best friend, that is my PEN, cause it's know everything about me, My first love is pizza,
My instagram I'd is s.cholera_13
My email address is s.cholera1304@gmail.com*

Soumya Swarup Nayak

I'm soumya Swarup Nayak
i'm from odisha
I write because I can't keep stranded in my mind
I'm doing my masters in zoology
I have dreams of writing novels and become a published author soon

My Instagram blog id is @wordsofsoumya

Tatsat Pandey

A future engineer having the passion of writing. Pursuing engineering in Btech @Electrical from MMMUT GKP

<u>VanshDeep Singh</u>

My name is Vanshdeep Singh, a class 11th student. I live in Basti(U.P.). Contact no. 6394535493

<u>Vishva Gajjar</u>

I'm Vishva Gajjar from Gujarat, Bhavnagar. I'm pursuing my master degree in English literature from MKBU. Writing makes me free from the chains of world and gives me my space to be myself.

Vivek Kumar shaw

Name- Vivek Kumar Shaw
Add- 2A Haridhan Dutta Lane cossipore Road
Kolkata- 700002
West Bengal
University- Mahatma gandhi antarrashtriya hindi vishwavidyalaya
Class- MA
Contact- 7685936321

ABOUT REASONS AND LAUGHTER

Reasons and Laughter is a community which deals with providing services, compiling anthologies, organising competitions and Open Mics, found by Japneet Kaur.

Our main objective is to give a good platform to budding writers to help them grow, even to provide best services and giving wings to their dreams.

Email: ralservicess@gmail.com

Instagram: @reasons_and_laughter